To Mani, thank you for showing us the wonders.

—ZF

To my mother, Rhonna Lesnie, who managed me when I was a difficult little baby.

And to Suzanne O'Sullivan, who managed me when I was a difficult little baby.

—PL

First published in Canada and the U.S. by Greystone Books in 2022
Originally published in Australia in 2021 by Hachette Australia Pty Ltd.
Text copyright © 2021 by Zana Fraillon
Illustrations copyright © 2021 by Phil Lesnie

22 23 24 25 26 5 4 3 2 1

Greystone Kids / Greystone Books Ltd.
greystonebooks.com

Cataloguing data available from Library and Archives Canada
ISBN 978-1-77840-008-7 (cloth)
ISBN 978-1-77840-009-4 (epub)

Proofreading by Doeun Rivendell
The illustrations in this book were rendered in watercolor.

Printed and bound in Singapore on FSC® certified paper at COS Printers Pte Ltd
The FSC® label means that materials used for the product have been responsibly sourced.

Greystone Books gratefully acknowledges the Musqueam, Squamish, and Tsleil-Waututh peoples
on whose land our Vancouver head office is located.

Greystone Books thanks the Canada Council for the Arts, the British Columbia Arts Council, the Province of British
Columbia through the Book Publishing Tax Credit, and the Government of Canada for supporting our publishing activities.

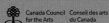

The Curiosities

GREYSTONE KIDS

GREYSTONE BOOKS · VANCOUVER/BERKELEY/LONDON

ZANA FRAILLON   PHIL LESNIE

The Curiosities came at dawn.
By the time Miro woke, they had
already chosen their nesting space.

At first, the Curiosities were quiet.
They blended in.

At first, Miro didn't even notice
them, perched on his shoulders
and nuzzled in his hair.

At first, Miro thought the tingle
he felt was just the warmth of the
sun or the murmuring of the wind.

But slowly, Miro began to see things differently.

He began to feel things differently, and do things differently too.

The Curiosities would point and chirp and pull him toward places
hidden away from everyday eyes. They showed him how to swim
with the stars and tickle the songs from the earth.

They showed him how to whisper
up waves and weave clouds to make
stories for the wind.

Miro had never noticed
all the oddments and
snippets before, all those
wonders and possibles
waiting in the shadows
where no one else looked.

And when the night whispered its song across the earth, and Miro could feel the Curiosities prickling inside him, he would play his fiddle. The Curiosities would cheer and clap, the music becoming more wild and more wonderful than he could ever imagine. Then Miro and his Curiosities would dance and play deep into the night.

Before long, others began to notice the Curiosities too.
When Miro guided a weathered elder to her home, her
hand soft on his arm and her world-wrinkled stories
gentle in his ear, he smiled as she patted the head of a
Curiosity, perched and listening to her words.

But sometimes, the Curiosities were so loud
and strange that people couldn't help but stare.

The Curiosities trilled and gurgled, pulling at Miro's arms and flapping at his legs, whispering in his ears so that everything around him disappeared into a buzz of cold noise and confusion.

Sometimes, the Curiosities were so bright
and brilliant that everyone turned away.

Then, no matter what he did, Miro was invisible.

One evening, as the sun tiptoed across the very
tops of the trees, something itched at the Curiosities.
A wild, untamed storm, furious and strong.

The Curiosities gathered, cheering and clapping and stomping and yowling. Miro demanded quiet. He pleaded for peace. But the Curiosities would not be tamed.

They shrieked and roared.
They washed over Miro, loud and
strange and bright and brilliant
and prickly and tingly; flapping
and hissing and screeching and
hurtling. The darkness wrapped
itself around him, deep, black,
and wet. Miro howled.

He felt the ground vanish beneath him, and the sounds
of the earth fade, until all around him was deep silence.

Then he heard it. A whisper of a voice. Just a snippet of a world-wrinkled story, dancing on the wind. Miro uncurled. He opened his eyes.

And there it was. A single thread of
knowing, thin and fragile and almost
invisible to his fingers, but there.
Gently, carefully, Miro pulled.

And when the elder appeared, the ground grew again under Miro's feet, and the sounds of the earth broke through the hissed whispers of the Curiosities.

The elder helped Miro to his feet, brushing away the darkness. Miro could still feel the Curiosities itching, but he could feel the thread too. Getting stronger and harder to break.

Miro rubbed his eyes and blinked in the light. He hadn't realized how many threads had already grown.

Miro soon found that the more threads that grew, the easier it
was to shed the darkness when it came.

And even though strangers still sometimes stared, or turned away,
Miro had the knowing of many others.

And it seemed to Miro that the Curiosities had chosen lots of other people too, in lots of different ways.

From time to time, when the breeze blew just so across the mountains and a hint of rain cartwheeled on the air, the Curiosities would leave. Their wings would spread and they would soar high on the wind.

They always came back, but Miro didn't mind.

Now, Miro could swim with the stars and tickle the songs from the earth.
He could whisper up waves and weave clouds to make stories for the wind.

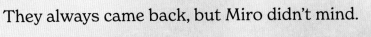

Now, Miro could see all the oddments and snippets, all those hidden wonders and possibles waiting in the shadows.

Can you?

FROM ZANA

When my child was five years old, they were diagnosed with Tourette's syndrome. Tourette's syndrome is a chronic neurological disorder that is characterized by rapid, repetitive, involuntary, and uncontrollable movements and sounds known as tics. For a person with Tourette's syndrome, trying not to tic is like trying not to blink. After a while, the urge is overwhelming.

People with Tourette's syndrome often also have other neurodiversities, such as ADHD, OCD, and anxiety disorders. Although dealing with neurodiversities and disability can be difficult, uncomfortable, and painful, the pathways and connections formed inside the brain to deal with these differences can enable people to perceive the world in insightful, understanding, and wondrously varied ways. My child is proud of their disability. It does not define them, but it is part of their identity, part of who they are.

While I wrote this book based on our experience of Tourette's syndrome, I hope it can equally be read as a story for anyone who feels different, anyone who feels lost and alone, and anyone who has been found.

I hope that *The Curiosities* can encourage all of us to embrace and celebrate diversity. People are disabled not by their disability or their difference, but by the barriers created by society. We are, all of us, united in our difference. Be proud.

FROM PHIL

In the folklore of the Philippines, where my mother comes from, there is an oral tradition of stories about *aswang*, which are shape-shifting, viscera-sucking ghouls and monsters. I find them terrifying—and utterly irresistible. There is the Tikbalang, a horse-headed trickster; and my personal favorite, the Lampong, a beardy little shape-shifter who assumes an animal form and leaps in front of flying arrows to save wild deer from hunters. There is the Kapre, a relatively benevolent tree giant who gives lousy directions. Oh, and then there's a . . . pig. A *really* big pig, who might be magical. I've never seen an *aswang* myself, but I'm still pretty sure they exist. It's why I chose to base Miro's Curiosities on them.

In portraying the elder who cares for Miro, I was drawn to the figure of the Babaylan in Philippine history. Babaylan were priestesses and community leaders, always female or female presenting, who had unique access to the spiritual world. Sometimes, a person was chosen to become a Babaylan when they began to exhibit neurodiverse traits such as Miro's—tics, seizures, depression, or hallucinations. These were signs that one had been selected by spirits, and crucially, the initiation rites of those Babaylan who exhibited these signs revolved around acceptance and answering the call of those spirits.

Using these to inspire me to paint Zana's story, I find it impossible not to wonder what it might be like for Miro to grow up in a place where brain differences actually afford someone political power, and where his tics, his Curiosities, are viewed as a communion with magic, essential in the life of a community.

ZANA FRAILLON has won and been shortlisted for some of the most prestigious prizes in children's literature. Her 2016 novel *The Bone Sparrow* won the ABIA Book of the Year for Older Children, the Readings Young Adult Book Prize, and the Amnesty CILIP Honour. It was also shortlisted for the Guardian Children's Fiction Prize, the Gold Inky Award, and the CILIP Carnegie Medal. Zana was inspired to write *The Curiosities* by her own neurodiverse child, and she lives in Melbourne, Australia.

PHIL LESNIE is a Sydney-based children's book illustrator and children's bookseller. He works primarily in watercolor because in a watercolor painting even mistakes look lovely. Phil is the illustrator of *Feathers*, which was shortlisted for the Prime Minister's Literary Awards in 2018. His first three books were CBCA Notables in 2015, 2016, and 2018. But his first cat, Cassidy, is notable all of the time.